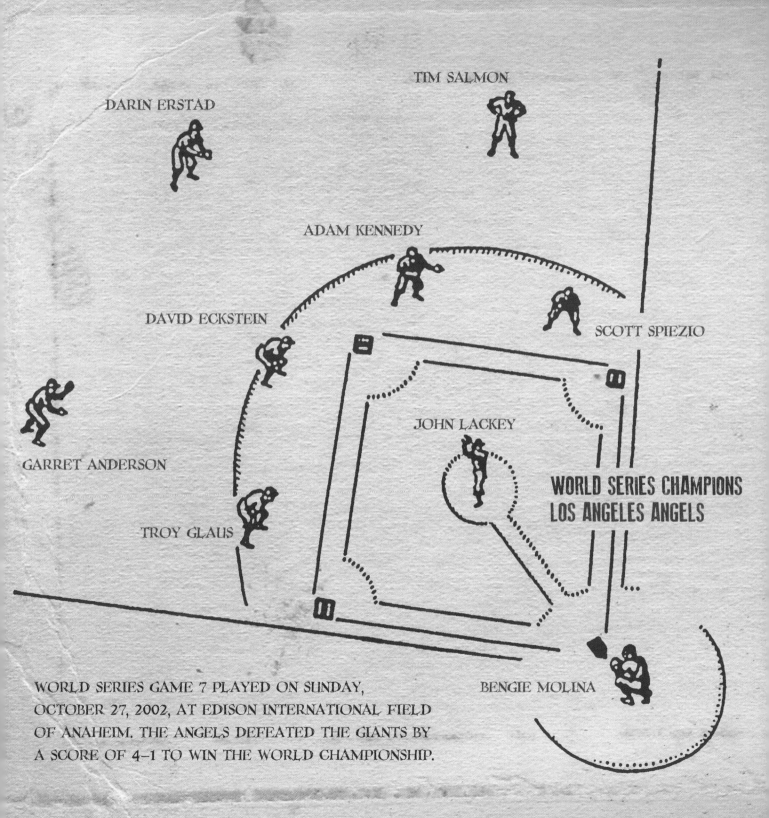

TIM SALMON

DARIN ERSTAD

ADAM KENNEDY

DAVID ECKSTEIN

SCOTT SPIEZIO

GARRET ANDERSON

JOHN LACKEY

WORLD SERIES CHAMPIONS
LOS ANGELES ANGELS

TROY GLAUS

BENGIE MOLINA

WORLD SERIES GAME 7 PLAYED ON SUNDAY,
OCTOBER 27, 2002, AT EDISON INTERNATIONAL FIELD
OF ANAHEIM. THE ANGELS DEFEATED THE GIANTS BY
A SCORE OF 4–1 TO WIN THE WORLD CHAMPIONSHIP.

LOS ANGELES ANGELS
OF ANAHEIM

SARA GILBERT

CREATIVE EDUCATION

Published by Creative Education
P.O. Box 227, Mankato, Minnesota 56002
Creative Education is an imprint of The Creative Company
www.thecreativecompany.us

Design and production by Blue Design (www.bluedes.com)
Art direction by Rita Marshall
Printed in the United States of America

Photographs by Getty Images (Doug Benc, Lisa Blumenfeld, Scott
Boehm, P Brouillet, Ralph Crane/Time & Life Pictures, Jonathan
Daniel, Diamond Images, Stephen Dunn, Don Emmert/AFP,
Focus on Sport, Otto Greule Jr, Leon Hulip, Scott Halleran, Jeff
Haynes/AFP, David Hofmann, Harry How, Kurt Hutton/Picture
Post, Walter Iooss Jr./Sports Illustrated, Jed Jacobsohn, V.J. Lovero,
Ronald Martinez, Rich Pilling/MLB Photos, Mike Powell, Louis
Requena/MLB Photos, Rogers Photo Archive), National Baseball
Hall of Fame Library, Cooperstown, N.Y.

Library of Congress Cataloging-in-Publication Data
Gilbert, Sara.
Los Angeles Angels of Anaheim / Sara Gilbert.
p. cm. — (World series champions)
Includes bibliographical references and index.
Summary: A simple introduction to the Los Angeles Angels of
Anaheim major league baseball team, including its start in 1961, its
World Series triumphs, and its stars throughout the years.
ISBN 978-1-60818-265-7
1. Los Angeles Angels (Baseball team)—History—Juvenile
literature. I. Title.
GV875.A6G55 2013
796.357'640979496—dc23   2011051184

First edition
9 8 7 6 5 4 3 2 1

Cover: Pitcher Jered Weaver
Page 2: Center fielder Torii Hunter
Page 3: Pitcher Bartolo Colón
Right: Angel Stadium

LF

BRIAN DOWNING

1B

WALLY JOYNER

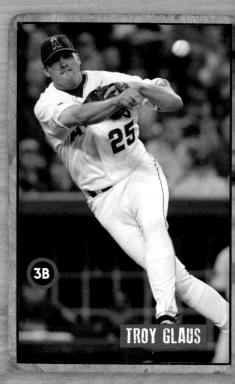

3B

TROY GLAUS

P

BRENDAN DONNELLY

RF

GARRET ANDERSON

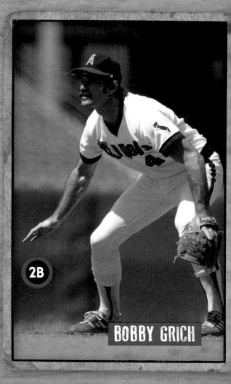

2B

BOBBY GRICH

TABLE OF CONTENTS

LOS ANGELES AND ANGEL STADIUM

Los Angeles is the second-biggest city in America. More than 3 million people live there. Los Angeles is also home to a ballpark called Angel Stadium. The Los Angeles Angels of Anaheim play baseball games there.

RIVALS AND COLORS

The Angels are a major league baseball team. They play against other major-league teams to win the World Series and become world champions. The Angels' colors are red, white, and blue. Their main **RIVALS** are another California team, the Oakland A's.

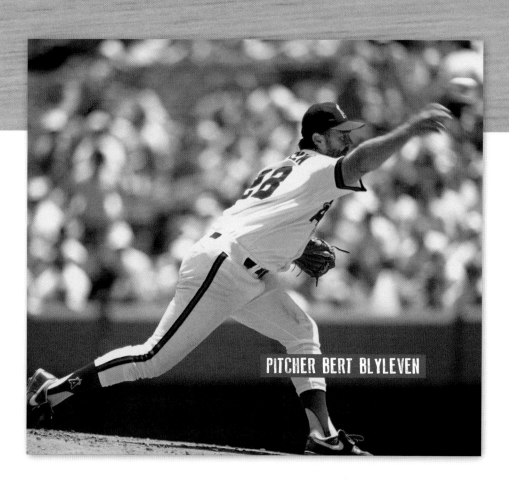

PITCHER BERT BLYLEVEN

LEFT FIELDER DON BAYLOR

PITCHERS KEN McBRIDE

ANGELS HISTORY

The Angels played their first season in 1961. Pitcher Dean Chance helped the team win many games. They got better almost every season. But the Angels had to wait a long time to get to the PLAYOFFS.

In 1972, star pitcher Nolan Ryan joined the Angels. His fiery fastball helped the

DEAN CHANCE

BO BELINSKY

CF

DARIN ERSTAD

RF

REGGIE JACKSON

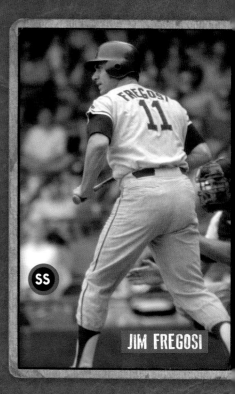

SS

JIM FREGOSI

P

BARTOLO COLÓN

P

JERED WEAVER

SS

ERICK AYBAR

NOLAN RYAN

Angels reach the playoffs for the first time in 1979. The Angels made it to the playoffs in 1982 and 1986, too. But they could not reach the World Series.

Angels fans waited 16 more years before the team got back to the playoffs. In 2002, **ROOKIE** pitcher Francisco Rodriguez

VLADIMIR GUERRERO

helped the Angels get to the World Series. Then they beat the San Francisco Giants to win their first world championship! Manager Mike Scioscia and powerful outfielder Vladimir Guerrero made sure the Angels stayed one of the best teams. They returned to the playoffs several times but did not get back to the World Series.

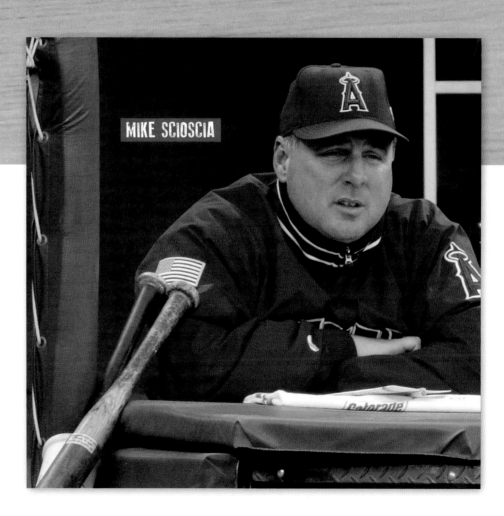

MIKE SCIOSCIA

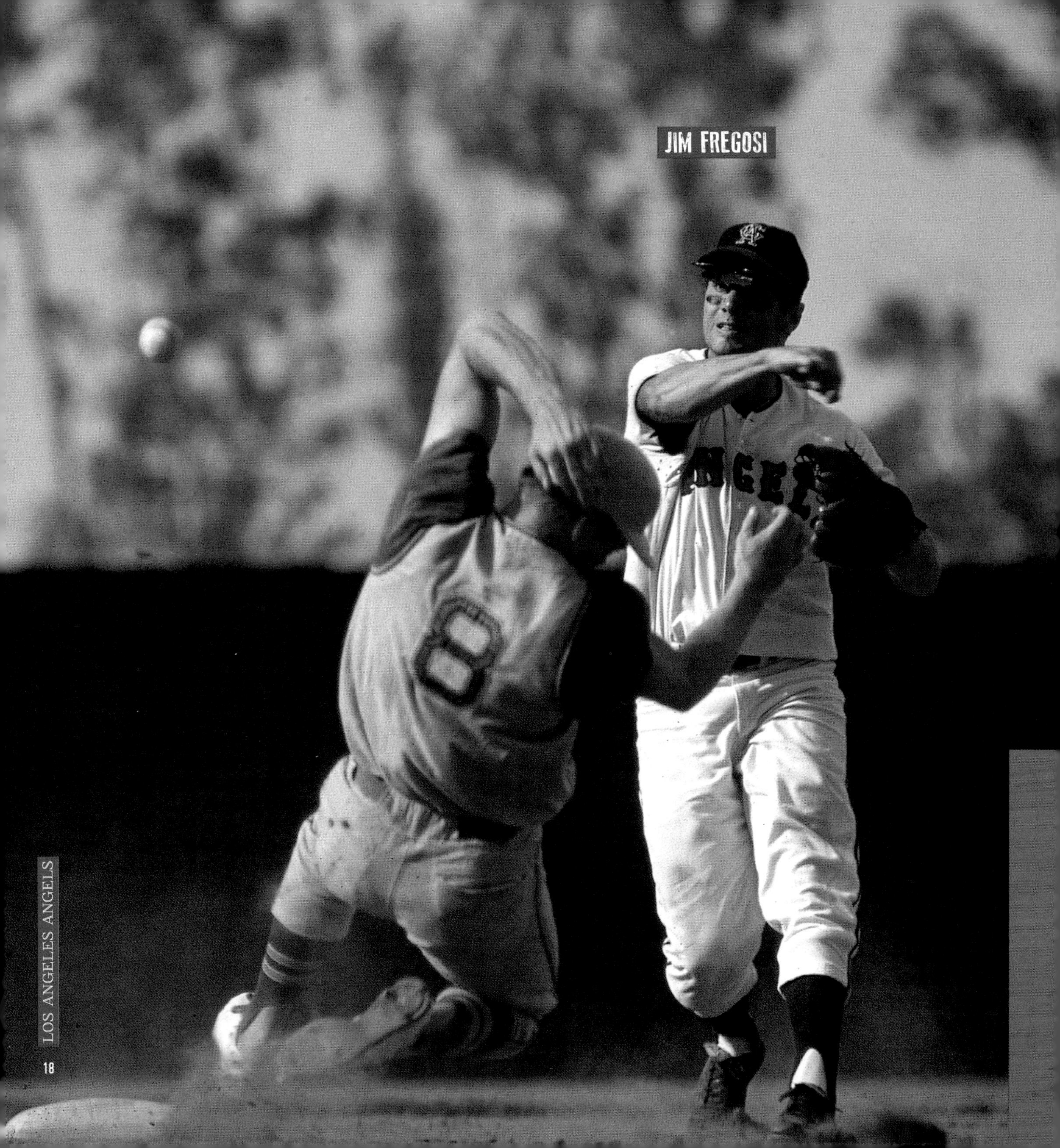

JIM FREGOSI

ANGELS STARS

Shortstop Jim Fregosi was a fan favorite in Los Angeles from 1961 to 1971. He became manager in 1978. Sweet-swinging first baseman Rod Carew hammered hits all over the field for the Angels in the 1980s.

Powerful **CLOSER** Troy Percival joined the Angels in 1995. He helped the Angels win hundreds of games. Slugging third baseman Troy Glaus had a mighty swing. He hit 47 home runs in 2000.

In 2006, Jered Weaver became one of the Angels' best pitchers. His **CHANGEUP** struck out a lot of batters. Fans hoped his strong arm would help the Angels win a second World Series soon!

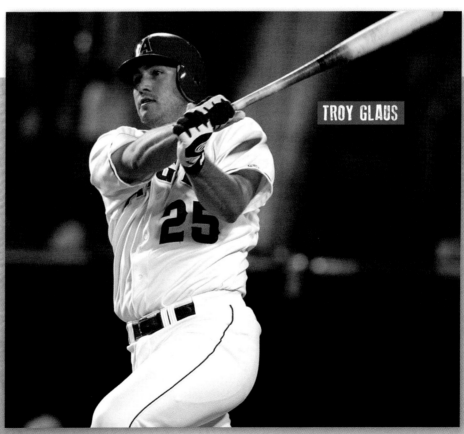

TROY GLAUS

JERED WEAVER

HOW THE ANGELS GOT THEIR NAME

The Angels were named for the city in which they play. Los Angeles is Spanish for "the angels." A Los Angeles minor-league baseball team used to be called the Angels, too. The owners of the new Angels had to pay the other team's owner $300,000 to use the name.

ABOUT THE ANGELS

First season: 1961

League/division: American League, West Division

World Series championship:

2002   4 games to 3 versus San Francisco Giants

Angels Web site for kids:

http://mlb.mlb.com/ana/fan_forum/kids_club.jsp

Club MLB:

http://web.clubmlb.com/index.html

GLOSSARY

CHANGEUP — a pitch that looks fast to a batter but is actually slow

CLOSER — a pitcher who usually pitches the last inning of a game

PLAYOFFS — all the games (including the World Series) after the regular season that are played to decide who the champion will be

RIVALS — teams that play extra hard against each other

ROOKIE — an athlete playing his or her first year

INDEX